THE *Amazon* RIVER AND ITS MAJOR TRIBUTARIES

Rain Forest Area

Mountain Area

The Amazon has two headstreams that originate in the Andes, the Marañon and the Ucayali, which are thought of as part of the Amazon proper. The streams join just above Iquitos, Peru, to form a waterway navigable by large ships. The slope of the last several hundred miles of the river's descent to the Atlantic is so slight that high tide is experienced far inland. The Amazon is about 4000 miles long, about 200 miles shorter than the Nile. It is called the world's mightiest river because it carries a much larger volume of water than any other.

For Mom, of course—J.H.G.

For Cheryl Lyne—J.P.

Clarion Books a Houghton Mifflin Company imprint 215 Park Avenue South, New York, NY 10003. Printed in the U.S.A. Library of Congress Cataloging-in-Publication Data Gilliland, Judith Heide. River / by Judith Heide Gilliland ; illustrated by Joyce Powzyk. p. cm. Summary: Describes the multifaceted Amazon River and the life it supports in its rain forests. ISBN 0-395-55963-4 1. Natural history—Amazon River Region—Juvenile literature. 2. Amazon River—Juvenile literature. [1. Amazon River. 2. Natural history—Amazon River Region. 3. Rain forests.] I. Powzyk, Joyce Ann, ill. II. Title. QH112.G56 1992 508.81'1—dc20 91-23870 CIP AC HOR 10 9 8 7 6 5 4 3 2 1

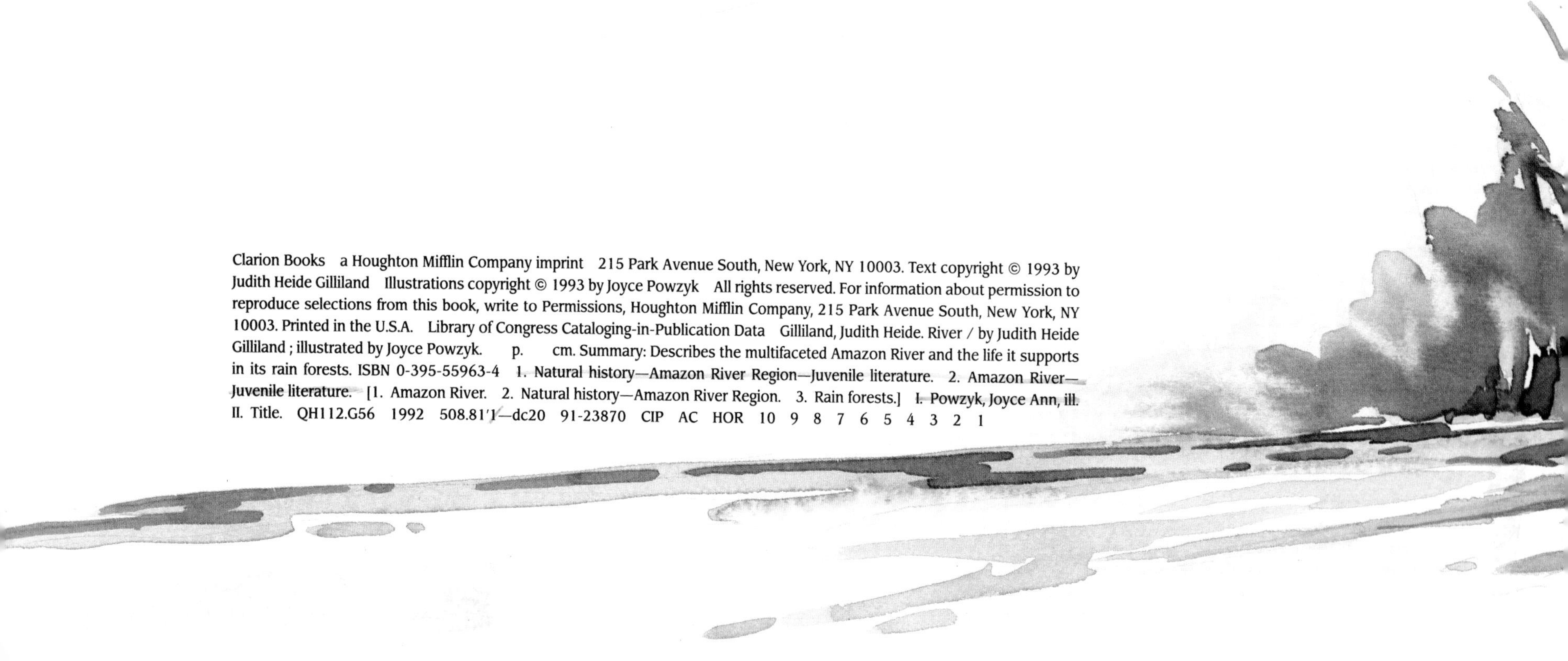

JUDITH HEIDE GILLILAND

River

Illustrated by
JOYCE POWZYK

CLARION BOOKS
New York

This is a story about a river,
the mightiest river in the world.
Its name is Amazon.

It is born high in the mountains, a cold trickle
no wider than a baby's foot.

Snow melts, rain falls, other streams from far away
hurry to meet it. It grows larger and larger.
It twists and turns like one of its great snakes.

It falls, and its falling makes
waterfalls and rainbows.
It is fast and rough and loud.
People call it The Great Speaker.

It is slow and smooth and quiet.
People call it The River Sea.

Strange and wonderful fish swim in its water:
Razor-toothed piranhas
and shocking electric eels
and sharp-faced needlefish
and (yes!) ferocious sharks
and secret and mysterious creatures
only the river knows about.

As it rushes to the sea it rushes to the skies,
becoming clouds,
raining each afternoon,
bringing life to forests.
The forests grow for a thousand miles
in every direction.
They are so damp and so wet
that the trees themselves rain.
They are called rain forests.

[redacted]

And in these rain forests
live jaguars,
and anacondas,
and giant anteaters.

Here herons rest in trees.
They look like great white flowers.
They take flight.
Who sees them?

Other birds see them.
And tapirs do.
And capybaras do.

And so do a hundred hundred eyes
that watch and wait
in the forest. . . .

The forest, with its green wet trees. . . .
Their leaves touch other leaves high up
to make a giant roof.

Even in the daytime it is dark and silent.
There is not a sound.
Except
BOOM,
the fruit of the Cannon Ball tree
crashes to the ground.
SSSSSSSSS, army ants march across fallen leaves.
Tffffffffft, a bird is caught in a giant spiderweb.

It is quiet again.

But listen! High up in the trees, there at the top,
don't you hear something?
There, where the sun shines, is a treetop world:
Monkeys chatter and play and swing by their tails.
They live up there, near the sunlight.
They do not visit the dark forest floor.
Maybe they do not even know it is there.

The parrots talk, the howler monkeys howl,
and in the evening the vampire bats flit
across the dark spaces.
Down on the ground a jaguar growls.
And the slow sleepy sloth turns its head.

Most of them no one has ever seen.

And the insects!
Huge mosquitoes
and enormous beetles
and bugs—bugs that look like flowers
and sticks
and great staring eyes—
and butterflies as big as a man's back.

And there are old riddles here, too:
old and important riddles.
It is strong but it is fragile.
It is famous, but no one knows it.
People need it, but they destroy it.

It is the Amazon—
river, forests,
clouds, and rain.
And more.

And more.